Who paid for the bullet?

A Mystery Short Story

for me

Who paid for the bullet?

A Mystery Short Story

TOPAZ HAUYN

ISBN: 9798408886241
Font: Alegreya
Coverdesign: Topaz Hauyn
Art: vectomart/depositphotos.com

The plastic surface of the rectangular smartphone was cold in my hand. The glass felt even colder against my ear.

I stood in front of my blue, old car. It served me for over a decade now. Reliable.

But the white plastic bag, knotted at the exterior mirror, was not mine.

I stood alone in the parking area of my company. Nobody else was around at this time of the day.

Cool air made my chill deeper.

"You kill the man with the round glasses", said the female voice on the other side of the phone. "Else you'll lose your husband."

I gulped. Fear running through my body, shaking my hands.

I'd call the police immediately, I decided. Moved my finger on the screen to the replacement icon.

"Don't think about the police. They will never believe you, with the weapon hanging on your car door", said the female voice. Without any accent, but in perfect academic tone.

"Yes", I said, coaxing the word through fear-stricken lips.

The headlines in the newspaper told Jem Maissner about the death of his former boss William Smith.

He sat in the seat of the suburban train to his workplace. The newspaper was folded in half in his hands, to read the article on top without spreading the whole size over his neighbors sitting next and opposite to him on equally blue seats.

The rattling of the tires on the tracks provided a constant rocking in the dark tunnel, that flew by outside the window. The yellowish lights of the suburban train lit the coach.

He felt his backpack rock against his shin in rhythm with the rattling.

Jem smelled the stale, cold air filled with the stench of coffee cups in the hands of the many rush hour fellow guests, although he did his best to breathe through his mouth alone.

The only reason he didn't drive to work by car was the jam on the roads. He would need four times the time he needed by suburban train.

He heard yawns around him. From somewhere hammered loud beats. Probably a person with earphones and music tuned way too loud.

Jem reread the headline, blinking twice.

He had read it right the first time. William Smith, owner of Smith Consulting in Stuttgart, Germany, was killed. Shot on Saturday night walking from his black, expensive Porsche car to his house's front door.

Nothing stolen.

William Smith's round glasses, destroyed and trampled to little shards.

No reason known.

Murderer on the run.

Of course, nothing stolen, thought Jem sarcastically. Nobody needed to kill a man to steal a Porsche. There were enough of them around in the region. A lot of them more expensive than William's Panamera 4.

So, why would anyone want to kill him? Or destroy the cheap round glasses without a frame?

William had always been a fair boss. The company was profitable, the customers happy.

The constant rocking of the train slowed down. The wheels shrieked, slowing down the suburban train even more. Lights from outside came through the windows opposite the aisle of Jem's place.

Metro station Rotebühl Platz.

Jem folded his newspaper and grabbed his black backpack that stood between his feet on the floor.

He wriggled his way out of the window place, through the full aisle to the doors as much as possible.

Many people in cloth pants, shirts, dark jackets and black backpacks stood around him. Scenting of fresh showers and different perfumes. Much like himself with his black cloth pants, blue shirt and navy jacket, being fresh showered.

A new workweek begun.

Some faces were already familiar to Jem.

Not from knowing the people or ever speaking to them. Just form taking the same way to work with the suburban train each day. Like the huge blond woman with the huge earring dangling from her ears, or the thin, student-like man always wearing a checked scarf, even in summer.

The moment the suburban train came to a halt and the doors opened, Jem walked out with everyone, aiming for the stairs to escape the warm, stuffy air of the metro station. He never waited in the line for the moving staircase.

Doves flew past him through the metro station.

It would be going to be interesting to find out whether the company survived William's death.

The car smelled of glue and plastic. With less than five thousand kilometers mileage, it was almost factory-fresh.

"I told you to make it nondescript!", said the female voice. "Everything calls, 'look here', instead."

The voice was even, cold and undecipherable to me.

The repeated beep of the phone told me she cut the line.

When I tried to put down the phone, my hands shook violently. The phone fell in the slit between the passenger seat and the central console.

A man, with dark facial hair, a wrinkled blue shirt and blue tie, sat next to Eva at the round reception desk. A police officer in civilian clothes.

Jem saw them already from outside the sliding glass doors.

He was sure of his assumption of the man, because nobody ever sat next to Eva. She was working alone at the reception desk, doing some administration stuff, sorting papers and the like.

He walked through the self-opening doors with the newspaper still in his hand.

The light blue carpet, leading to the wall of white glass with stainless steel poles at the side, shielding Eva's paperwork from the new arrivals, absorbed the sound of his steps. The fountain over at the seating area for visitors filled the hall with an unnerving, constant rush.

"Good morning, Eva", said Jem. "What's today for breakfast? Vanilla cakes?"

He smiled at the blond woman with the brown eyes, who had a huge stack of paperwork in front of her.

"Good morning, Jem. Sure. Have one", said Eva. She picked up one of the round vanilla cakes and handed it over the little shelf at the top of the desks white glass wall.

The sweet scent of vanilla filled the air. That was way better than the air in the suburban train.

"Who are you?", asked the man next to Eva.

"Jem, this is police officer Edward Maier", said Eva. Pointing at the newspaper in Jem's hand she added: "Surely you know about William. Mr. Maier is here to interview all employees."

Jem looked around. The surveillance cameras still hung at the two corners behind him, watching and listening to everything that happened in the entrance hall.

He bites into Eva's cake. The sweet short cake decomposed under his teeth. He chewed slowly, enjoying each bit of the cake's flavor of vanilla, sugar and short consistence he could.

"I'm Jem Maissner. Working as a programmer at the new software we're about to publish next month", said Jem. He hesitated a moment, "in case the company continues to exit." He let his voice trail off.

Mr. Maier nodded and wrote something on his notepad.

"Thank you, Mr. Maissner. Any ideas who might want to see Mr. Smith dead?", asked Mr. Maier.

Jem shook his head. He knew nobody personally with a grudge against Mr. Smith.

"Fine. If something comes to your mind, Eva has my phone number", said Mr. Maier.

Jem nodded, took another one of the delicious vanilla cakes from Eva and walked through the next door, down the aisle with the white walls. His work waited. Or at least, he hoped so.

The little round cake was still in his hand as he opened the white door to the office he had his workplace.

His three colleagues were already there. Usually he was first at work.

"Good morning", said everyone. But the greetings sounded thin.

Jem could feel the insecurity hanging over all of them.

William Smith had been the single owner of Smith Consulting. With him gone, there was the procurator in charge. But the decisions on how to continue would be made by the heirs. Whoever they were.

His head spun.

Who wanted to see Mr. Smith dead? He wanted to know himself. But the most important thing to him today was the evening, when his beloved wife would return to him.

Jem returned to his home later than he wanted to. The suburban train was late, for somebody had thrown himself on the tracks.

He shuddered at the thought of doing such a stupid thing. Couldn't those people just find a silent corner, instead of causing mayhem at rush hour?

He put his keys on the brown surface of the phone cupboard next to the entrance door, slipped out of his shoes and hung his black jacket on the hanger. The church tower bell rung half past six in the evening outside. It's sound carrying through the windows audible though.

The air in the hall was warm and stale.

Jem was tired from the workday.

Nobody knew anything, but the gossip factory ran on full blast. Focusing on the stupid detail about the widow who claimed of knowing nothing. Or so she was quoted.

He walked through the kitchen, living room and bedroom opening all windows to let in fresh air.

Someone knew more than the others.

Jem was pretty sure the police didn't give away information they already had. This police officer called Mr. Maier hadn't been very informative this morning.

When Jem left work, both Mr. Maier and Eva had vacated the reception desk at the companies entrance hall.

Stefanie, his wife, hadn't been home yet.

The phone rang.

I heard it clearly. Too afraid about what would happen next, I parked at the side of the road, glad my fingers were able to stop the car.

Trying to reach the phone in the slit between the passenger seat and the central console I opened the seat belt. I couldn't reach it.

I felt my t-shirt cling wet at my whole body from my sweat. I could smell the sour taste of sweat, filled the whole car with my fear. I shivered.

Turning off the car had turned off the heating too.

I breathed relieved when the ringing stopped. Saved from another talk with this awful woman who had forced me to kill a man.

My cheeks got wet. Not from sweat, but from salty tears, running past my lips, tasting salty.

Restarting the car, I merged into the traffic rushing past me. The clock said it was half past six in the evening. My husband would be already waiting for me.

Hopefully he was alive.

∿❈∿

Jem sat on the dark green, soft, four-people-wide sofa in the living room with the white-painted wall at his back.

He couldn't relax. Instead, he tapped his fingers on the wooden surface of the desk in front of him.

The sudden business trip of Stefanie was uncommon. Being late wasn't that much. Probably she got stuck in a traffic jam.

He missed her soft body at his side during the night, her happy chatting during dinner and her long brown hair to wave through with his fingers.

For four days she had been away now.

A sudden need of replacement at a fair. Or so she told him.

Jem stared at the plate in front of him. Warmed-up green beans. He cooked them yesterday from the fridge and didn't eat them completely. Today, the béchamel sauce tasted thick and only like flour. He surely forgot an important spice, or maybe only water.

Instead of eating, Jem thought about his former boss. What an awful way to be shot in front of one's house.

And the only thing that wasn't like always on that Saturday afternoon, had been Stefanie's absence. At least for Jem.

He sighted, picked up the spoon and started eating the thick béchamel sauce with the delicious green beans.

⌇⌇⌇⊗⌇⌇⌇

Finishing his dinner, Jem heard a key unlocking the front door.

Joy of having her back ran through his body. He put the spoon aside, stood and walked through the door into the hall. Turning on the light.

Stefanie stood at the open door.

Jem smelled her sweat and saw her white blouse hanging wet around her from the bit her jacked revealed.

Her eyes had black circles under them, as if she hadn't slept this weekend.

"Hello, Sweetheart", said Jem.

He rushed past the kitchen door and pulled Stefanie in his arms, ignoring her purse.

She let it go, and he heard a hard, metallic clash on the floor.

"Welcome home", murmured Jem.

Stefanie felt stiff in his arms.

He stepped back half a step, without letting her go, and looked into her face.

"What's wrong, Sweetheart?", asked Jem.

And what was in her purs making such a sound, he wondered, but didn't ask.

Stefanie looked frightened to death.

"Hello, Jem", said Stefanie. "I'm home."

Her voice was thin.

"Want to take a shower first and then go to bed?", asked Jem. "You look exhausted."

Stefanie nodded.

⚙

Jem brought two purple towels, Stefanie's favorite color, to the bathroom, where she already stood under the shower.

The hot, running water filled the room with water fume. The transparent walls of the shower were already fogged.

He picked up her blouse to put it into the washing machine.

"Where's your suitcase?", asked Jem.

"Lost", said Stefanie over the rush of water splashing over her body before dripping in large drops to the porcelain shower base.

Jem stared at the white blouse in his hands. How could she lose her suitcase?

He turned the white fabric into a ball and stopped. There were red stains on one side. Unfolding the blouse, he inspected them closer. They weren't the deep, dark red coming from spilled wine, nor where they at the top of the blouse where one would expect them.

The stains were light red, blurred, at the hem of the blouse. The place usually stuffed into the trousers.

Jem stared at the fogged shower walls next to him.

Stefanie wasn't humming like she usually did during a shower. She shoved herself silent. No chatting about her day either.

"Forgot the new detergent in the shopping bag", murmured Jem.

He left the damp, hot, fogged bathroom with the blouse held tight in his fist.

In the hall with the fresher, cooler air, Jem inhaled deeply.

He walked to Stefanie's purse, picked it up and carried it to the living room.

It was heavier than usual, although he didn't know its usual contents. Never had any reason to search her purse, though.

Stefanie couldn't be the murder, could she? Where was the reason for this? She didn't even know William Smith more than by name as company owner.

Jem pushed his spoon and plate, with the cold remnants of the green beans with béchamel, aside. Then, placed the brown bag on the brown table surface.

Unzipping the cold metal zipper gave him a chill. The artificial fabric outside was smooth and cold under his fingers. It was wrong to search her bag. Fear for what he might discover kept him going though.

Jem searched the inside pockets at the side and the huge center. He found her purse, some candy she liked, handkerchiefs, a mirror, no phone and a gun.

He pulled the gun out.

He stared at it like he'd stare at a predator standing in front of him without a fence like in the zoo.

The lights from the ceiling reflected on the shiny metal that laid cold in his hand.

Afraid of the weapon he put it down on the table.

Fear trickled in beads of sweat over his forehead.

The digital clock in blue on his radio, standing next of the TV opposite the table, said it was seven o'clock.

Eva was long at home. No way he could get the phone number for the police officer from her now. Which police station should he call? Should he call any and loose Stefanie?

He listened, heard the faint rush of water. Good, she was still in the shower with the water running.

Jem crunched with his teeth.

He loved his wife. How could she murder anybody? Did she murder William?

The possession of a gun was no proof for a crime he reminded himself.

Yet, he knew of no other conclusion. Especially with her never on business trip. Urgent need on a fair suddenly sounded like a very thin reason.

The running water in the bathroom was disabled. Silence filled the room.

Jem made a quick decision.

He pulled his phone from his pair of trousers back pocket and dialed 110.

Jem heard Stefanie walking through the hall to their bedroom. She would take her time to dress, for her hair needed some combing after a shower and before she braided it to go asleep.

Precious minutes to call for help.

He wanted the gun out of his home as soon as possible. Throwing it out through the window or trashing it felt wrong though.

"Emergency switchboard, where is the place of action?", said a male voice.

Jem said his address as fast as he could, and his name. He added there was a gun and he thought a connection to William Smiths murder on Saturday. Then, he waited for further questions.

He looked at the gun on the table. Were there bullets in? He had no knowledge about weapons, so he couldn't tell. Alone having one in front of him scared him like hell.

The man at the other side of the line asked a question.

Jem didn't understand it, for Stefanie ts-tsked in front of him.

He looked up and stared into her face, red from the hot shower, but with uncombed hair.

He hadn't paid attention to Stefanie.

"That's not nice", said Stefanie.

Jem gulped. His lips felt dry. The voice of the man at the emergency switchboard asked something else. Jem couldn't follow.

He put his phone down on the table without breaking the line.

Stefanie stood in front of him. Dressed in her purple pajama, her eyes wide, shaking.

"What did you do, Stefanie? Why did you bring a gun in our home here at the Bach Street?", asked Jem.

Was it the address the dispatcher needed again?

He didn't know but went on, trying his best to find out more.

"Sweetheart, why are you shaking? What's wrong?", asked Jem.

Stefanie didn't answer at first, but then started talking. "I shot a man who wore glasses. She forced me, threatened to kill you if I didn't obey." Sobbing interrupted Stefanie's words.

Killing him? Shivers of ice ran over Jem's hands. He remembered the threats he got as e-mails at work. Threats to quit working for Smith Consulting if he liked his life.

He always deleted them as Spam without further comment. With so many misspelling, who could take them seriously?

"Who was she?", asked Jem.

He tried to remember the senders name on the e-mails, but couldn't. They were about half a year back.

"I don't know. A voice over the phone", said Stefanie. "I didn't listen, until last Thursday morning there was a gun in a bag knotted at the exterior mirror of my car."

Jem walked around the table, pulled Stefanie in his arms. Tried to calm her down a bit.

For he never felt calm, he stared at his phone. If the line was still active the dispatcher said no word.

Jem glanced around the room. The door to the hall stood half open. The table was littered with the gun, the purse, his smartphone and the dirty dishes. The TV and radio were on standby.

He looked through the window. There were no neighbors on the window at the next house. But without curtains, one could see him and Stefanie clearly.

She still sobbed in his arms. "I am so glad you're still alive."

"Shall we sit down?", asked Jem.

He pulled Stefanie down to the floor instead of to the sofa. If anybody observed them from the window next house, this person at least wouldn't see them anymore.

"Do you know who you shot?", asked Jem.

Shooting a person on a description basis of wearing glasses only seemed to thin to him.

Stefanie shook her head. "No. Just he was walking from a Porsche to an expensive mansion up the hill."

He thought her dangerous by this. "Why didn't you call the police? It's just dialing 110, you know", said Jem.

Which was the wrong thing to say, for Stefanie sobbed even more. The tears running from her eyes made her face a deep red.

His but went cold on the tiled floor. It was uncomfortable to sit there, leaned against the side of the sofa, holding Stefanie, waiting for the police to hopefully show up.

〰〰❈〰〰

My hair hung wet around my shoulders. Dripping on my favorite purple pajama.

How could Jem, my beloved husband, risk his life just calling the police, when I had done literally everything to save him? Even volunteering to go to prison myself!

The cold, tiled floor let my bare feet freeze.

I was glad my phone was still in my car, trapped under the passenger's seat. For sure I would get a phone call for my husband's betrayal.

I wrapped my arms around my shivering body.

Calling the police was the first thing she forbade me to do. I obeyed, too afraid of my life and my husbands.

He pulled me in his warm arms, and down, sitting on the floor. Did he see her in the neighbor's window?

Probably not. If she was there we would be dead already.

Now, sitting on the cold floor of our living rooms, his arms around me, trying to soothe me, asking me questions, I wasn't able to do more than cry. I cried for the joy of hugging him again.

Smelling his warm, a little sweaty scent of man and green beans.

Probably for the last time.

I snuggled closer to him, not caring his phone call was still active. Maybe it would help the police catch her. Save the life of others.

The police would find me one way or the other, no need to hide my doing.

But how could I keep my husband save? Keep him alive to wait for me until I was released from prison sometime in the far future?

The doorbell brought back the cold, harsh reality.

It was the police, wasn't it? It couldn't be her.

Please not.

〰〰❁〰〰

The high ding dang dong of the doorbell, sounding like a little bell, echoed through the hall into the living room.

Jem had always loathed the sound, but Stefanie found it lovely, so he had let it be.

He loosened his embrace around Stefanie, to get up and open the door. This had to be the police he had called. They were quick. He liked that.

But Stefanie grabbed his arm with both hands. She didn't let go as his pulled gently.

Her eyes were huge and filled with blank fear of who might stand outside.

"It's alright", said Jem. "I'll find you a lawyer who will help you. We'll find the woman threatening you into murdering my former boss."

"Your manager?", asked Stefanie. Her voice was hoarse from the sobbing.

Jem nodded. "William Smith, the founder and owner of the consulting company I work for."

The doorbell rung again multiple times.

"I'll open. Let go", said Jem.

Stefanie held tighter. "No. It might be her", said Stefanie. "We're trapped."

She was right about the trap. There was no way out of their home aside from the door. Climbing out of a third floor window was a bad idea. As usual with the apartment buildings, there was no fire ladder.

Jem sighted.

"I won't know when I don't go looking", he said.

The doorbell was a constant ringing now. The high bell would crack from the overuse if it was a real one, thought Jem. He was glad, for the first time, that the bell was a recorded sound only, played when someone pressed the button.

Then, he heard heavy steps in front of their door. Probably heavy boots. Multiple steps.

"Police here. Open or we'll break the door", said a deep, probably male voice.

Jem felt Stefanie release her grip at the sound of the deep voice.

"Coming", called Jem.

He got up, walked over the cold tiled floor of the living room into the hall. Turned back on the light.

The ringing hadn't stopped.

Why would they continue ringing the doorbell?

Wondering he picked up the black receiver and answered the intercom.

"Yes, please?", said Jem.

The police on the other side of the door didn't move.

"Police here. You're Jem Maissner, calling us?", asked a dry voice.

"Yes. Third floor", said Jem.

He pressed the door opener button. Heard the buzz of the lock opening.

Something hit his home door with a crashing sound. A large crack run through his door.

"Help", shouted Jem into the receiver still in his hand.

A second hit crashed the door open. Bits and pieces of wood flew at him. He stumbled back, covering his eyes.

In front of him stood a person in black clothes, sturdy boots and a vicious smile on her lips.

Gun in hand.

Jem rubbed his eyes. The dust from the broken door blurred his sight.

He leaned against the door frame with the open kitchen door to his left.

"Naughty boy. Calling the police was a bad idea", said a female voice.

He saw the person lifting the gun and let himself drop to the left into the kitchen.

He heard a bang.

His arm hurt.

She shot him.

He ran past the oven, the fridge and the stove.

He turned, faced the countertop with the brown bambus knife block, grabbed the large kitchen knife.

His upper arm throbbed from pain. Something warm ran down his shirt.

Jem refused to check.

The police was downstairs. He just needed more time.

Breath, he ordered himself. Breath and defend yourself.

This woman was the real murderer.

In the hall, he heard her stomps step by step down the hall from her heavy boots.

Would she go after him, or straight to the living room after Stefanie? He hadn't heard a sound from her. Hopefully she hid behind the sofa.

One more step and she could try shooting him again from the sound of the steps.

Jem leaned back against the stove and crouched down. This was the side of the room nearer to the entrance door. If the woman shoot around the edge, she would probably aim for the countertop. And higher for his head.

At least he hoped so.

Jem held his healthy arm with the knife raised, ready to throw the knife.

"Stop. Police. Don't move", ordered a foreign voice.

"Stupid idiot", said the female voice.

Steps turned, another shot.

Jem heard a cry of pain. That wasn't the female faking a male again. She must have struck the police man.

He got up and slid sideways to the door as silently as possible. The throbbing pain in his arm hurt. He felt how his sight started to get blurry at the edge.

"Leave, or you'll follow your colleague", said the female voice, Jem hated by the very sound.

He peeked around the door frame.

The back of the murderer was to him. He couldn't see what or who was at the door, for she blocked his sight. He needn't to see. Knowing there was a standing police man was good enough for him.

Jem made another step with his raised knife, built up momentum and stabbed the black clad woman, who broke into his home, in her lower back where he estimated were no more ribs. He knew there were many vulnerable organs.

Keeping his knifes sharp for clean cuts on vegetables, he wasn't that surprised he hit and sliced her jacket, clothes and skin. But the knife went through her body like he was cutting overripe strawberries from the sound of her cry.

Surprised and still wondering, Jem didn't take care of the woman's reaction.

She hit him on the head with something hard. Probably with her gun.

Holding tight to the handle of the knife, Jem fell to the concert of a painful cry.

Jem's sight was a blur of black shades.

One cry was his own.

<hr>

He was rocked back and forth, left and right.

Jem tried to clear his head.

His surrounding smelled aseptic, like a hospital.

Yet, he was moved around, heard tires rolling and breaks slowing them down.

Somebody talked to another person next to him. He could feel the warmth of another person against his leg.

Where they sitting around him?

He couldn't open his eye or move a limb, for he was strapped on the soft table or hard bed or whatever he was on.

His upper arm still hurt, but the warm feeling of liquid running over it was gone.

A hand touched his forehead.

Stefanie's hand. He knew her slender fingers with the calluses at her fingertips from the huge amount of typing she did. He had none of them. Although, at work he did his fair amount of typing too.

"You'll be better, soon", said Stefanie's voice. "Sleep. The murderer is caught."

Jem wanted to know what would happen to her. He tried to ask, but his mouth felt try, his tongue heavy.

He couldn't form a word.

"Sleep. I'll stay with you until you wake up", said Stefanie.

Her reassuring voice reached him.

Jem relaxed and fell back asleep. Things would be put right.

I watched my husband relax under my touch.

The paramedic next to me nodded. I hoped it was approval.

They explained to me earlier, that my husband would live. A graze and a concussion.

I leaned back against the hard wall of the ambulance coach. Everything was white, while I felt myself black and guilty.

The police had taken my testimony and allowed me to go with my husband to the hospital. Under the requirement of accepting a police man there, making sure I didn't go on the run.

Watching my husband fight the straps I was glad it was over. The only open question, the why, wasn't sure to be answered. The woman's knife wound was grave.

I liked knowing he hit her badly.

THE END

Excerpt:
The One Time Chance

Tunja signed the last cream-white paper document of forty-something. The black pen in her hand was slippery from her sweat and the warmth of her hand. She clutched the pen hard to keep it between her thumb and index finger. Both burned from the unused exercise.

Heck her whole hand hurt as if each bone was set on fire.

"Tunja Reckmir" stood in red ink on the dotted line, written in a spidery signature. Compared to her signature on the first document, which was clean, elongate and beautiful, this one seemed to be done from a different person.

Come to think of it. She was a different person now.

Plotting the death of her victim in detail. Laying it out in multiple dozen documents. Adding reasons and argumentation about the why's, how's and when's. An exhausting exercise.

Yet, an important one. For her.

She wanted to live her live freely afterwards.

Without filling out all the paperwork she would be sent to prison for killing her neighbor Max Willmer tomorrow night with a knife. She chose to kill him during his sleep to give him no chance for defense. Taking the night after getting the permission for the murder would rob him of the time to set up any defense.

Tunja thought about the five pages she had filled in about how she thought Mr. Willmer would react to the message of his murder. To her observation during the last five years, Mr. Willmer was a man of habits. Habits he refused to break. Even, if it would cause others extra work like snow shoveling during winter. He did it at seven in the morning at twelve before lunch and after dinner at eight in the evening. No matter the real snow. Even if the sun shone and everything was dry.

Tunja remembered the pain, when she slipped at ten in the morning on a day with heavy snowfall. Her left leg and right arm were broken.

She gritted her teeth. Half a year of hard work and exercises was needed after the healing to be back walking around, living on her own.

Revenge, Tunja thought, revenge would help her live through this. Mr. Willmer hadn't even sent an apology, let alone asked if she needed help. A walker had found her and called the ambulance last winter.

Tunja shoved the sheets together in a neat heap, stuffed the wet pen into the outer pocket of her blue cotton blazer. Then she picked up the stack of forms and turned towards the open door.

Excerpt end of: The One Time Chance Ende der Leseprobe aus »Titel«

More books

Miriam loves to dress up and dine at a restaurant. Everyone at work asks her for recommendations.

Tired and on her red high heels she returns home. To find a commercial about a recently opened restaurant.

Recently? And she hadn't been there already? The name, "lost face restaurant" indicates a horror story. She hates those.

Will Miriam go? Will she like the food? Accompany her on a mysterious evening full of unexpected decisions.

Travel by train. Wish a travel nighbor away.
Wake up in a murder scene.

Petra travels by train. To Stuttgart to enjoy her holiday, visit they vineyards and tour the city. Relax. The travel strains her. Her travel neighbor reads the newspaper. Depressing headline after headline. Hopefully he detrains soon, wishes Petra.

A wish leading into a murder mystery nightmare. Not only her holidy, but also her freedom is at stake.

Mind your thoughts. They might come true in an ugly way.

Fantasy

Beaten Path in the Mist
Vampire Hunting with the Tiger Eye
Marlene's New Monster
Remorse of the Mermaid
Wipe off the Dust
The Book Burning
Stars Flying into Philosophy
Red: #890000

The True Mage Survives
The Flower on the Mountain Top
The speaking Mirror
The Fork with the Scales
Fairy Needs Courage
The Rainbow Bubble Collapse
Repair the Music
The missing Jack O'Lantern

Science Fiction

Abandonned Time Travel
Alien Visit
Coloring an Apple
Corrupted Food Storage
Dicovery (Novel)
Red: #890000
Served like red Wine
Shards of her Life

Support Refused
Sweet Depths
The Water Theft
Lottery Win: The Third Set of Doors
Human Interactions Preferred
Intertwined Fate

Mystery

Eating Out Adventure
Life Changing Game
The Lady Says: Die
The One Time Chance

Intertwined Fate
If date equals…
Keyring
Who paid for the bullet?